AMERICAN DREAMS

by Lisa Banim

SILVER MOON PRESS
NEW YORK

AMERICAN DREAMS
by Lisa Banim
Copyright © 1993 by Lisa Banim
First paperback edition 1995

For information contact
Silver Moon Press
New York, New York
(800) 874-3320

First Edition
Designed by John J. H. Kim
Printed in the United States of America

Cover photograph courtesy of
the Library of Congress

Library of Congress Cataloging-in-Publication Data

Banim, Lisa, 1960-
    American Dreams / by Lisa Banim. -- 1st ed.
    p. cm. -- (Stories of the States)
    Summary: Developments in World War II force Amy
Mochida and her family to move from Hollywood to an
internment camp with other Japanese Americans, changing
Amy's friendship with eleven-year-old Jeannie.
    ISBN 1-881889-34-3 (hardcover): $14.95
    ISBN 1-881889-68-8 (paperback): $5.95
    1. World War. 1939-1945--United States--Juvenile fiction.
[1. Japanese Americans--Evacuation and relocation.
1942-1945--Fiction. 2. World War. 1939-1945--United States-
-Fiction.] I. Title II. Series
PZ7.B2253Am   1993
[Fic]--dc20

                                        93-22573
                                            CIP
                                            AC

STORIES OF THE STATES

TABLE OF CONTENTS

CHAPTER ONE
"We're Safe Here in California"

"Hey, Jeannie, wait for me!" Eleven-year-old Jeannie Bosold turned around quickly. Her best friend, Amy Mochida, was hurrying toward the corner where the Hollywood streetcar stopped, her short black hair flying in her face.

"I changed my mind," Amy said as she came up. She was all out of breath. "I'm coming with you."

Jeannie gave her a big smile. "I knew you

would," she said. "Besides, you'd be crazy not to see the latest Barbara Cooper film. Everyone says it's just the best."

"Well, I want to see it, all right," Amy said. "But I sure don't want to get caught." She glanced nervously over her shoulder.

"Who's going to catch you?" Jeannie said. "Your mother is working, and we're not skipping school or anything. It's three o'clock already."

"I know," Amy said. "But I did tell my mother I was going to the library this afternoon."

"Well, my mother won't care," Jeannie said, tossing her blond curls. "She knows I've been dying to see *Fascinating Lady*."

Amy nodded. "Me, too," she said. "But I have to be home by dinnertime."

"No problem," Jeannie told her. "We don't have to stay for the whole show. The second feature is a war movie, anyway."

The Hollywood streetcar finally arrived,

and Jeannie and Amy got on. They had to walk all the way to the back to find a seat together.

Jeannie plopped down and took the latest copy of *Movie Life* magazine from her schoolbag. The cover read "September 1941." She flipped through it to the page she had marked with a bobby pin. "Take a look," she said, handing the magazine to Amy. She pointed to a photograph of a beautiful red-haired woman.

"It's Marianna Morgan!" Amy said excitedly.

"And she's standing right next to Clark Gable," Jeannie went on. "Her picture is in all the latest movie magazines."

Amy peered closely at the picture. "My mother made that pink suit," she said. "I remember her working on it."

Jeannie sighed. "You are so lucky, Amy. I mean, how many girls' mothers get to sew dresses for a real live actress?"

"Not many, I guess," Amy admitted. "But..."

"And I can't believe you actually live at Marianna Morgan's house," Jeannie went on dreamily. "Why, I'd just die for the chance to hang around a pool all day and talk to loads of glamorous people."

"That's not how it is at all," Amy said. "I keep trying to tell you that. It's actually kind of lonely. There aren't any other kids around, except Tad, the gardener's grandson. And Miss Morgan is always off somewhere, filming or making personal appearances. The only person who comes around all the time is that horrible old studio manager, Mr. Whick."

Jeannie took back the magazine. "Well, it sounds like a pretty good life to me," she said. "Just imagine, someday you can tell people you lived with Marianna Morgan. Maybe you'll even be interviewed by one of the Hollywood gossip columnists."

"Mmm," Amy replied. She gazed out the window as the streetcar clanked down Hollywood Boulevard. It was still very warm in late September, and the tall palm trees with their crowns of large green leaves were swaying in the slight breeze.

Jeannie had to nudge Amy when the streetcar reached their stop. "Come on," she said. "We're here."

They hopped off the streetcar and headed straight for the Kingsway Theater. A long line of people had already formed outside the gilded, red-domed building. The huge marquee read, "Today's Double Feature! Barbara Cooper in *Fascinating Lady* and John Randall in *The Guns of War!*" There was a huge poster of Barbara Cooper outside the theater. She looked very glamorous in a long red evening dress. The poster for *The Guns of War* showed a handsome young soldier leading his buddies into battle.

"War, war, war," Jeannie grumbled as she

and Amy took their places at the end of the line. "That's all anybody talks about these days, and our country isn't even fighting."

"Not yet," Amy said. "But so far no one has been able to stop Hitler and Mussolini from invading other countries."

Jeannie fumbled in her purse for change. "You mean in Europe," she said. "What does a war way over there have to do with us, anyway?"

"Weren't you paying attention in class today?" Amy asked, frowning. "Miss Gleason said this war has plenty to do with the United States. England and France were on our side in the last war, and now they need our help. Besides, who knows which country Hitler will invade next?"

"I suppose you're right," Jeannie said with a sigh. "Oh, look, the line is finally moving! Thank heavens!"

The girls bought their tickets from the lady in the little glass booth and walked into the theater.

"Wait, let's get some candy," Jeannie said. She hurried over to the refreshment counter. "Butter Rum Lifesavers," she told the girl. It was a brand new flavor, and she wanted to try it.

"I'll have a Tootsie Roll," Amy added.

"Five cents each," said the girl behind the counter. She sounded very bored.

A few moments later, a young usher dressed in a red uniform with gold braid on the shoulders and a round red hat took their tickets. "You want to sit in the balcony?" he asked.

Jeannie looked up at the balcony section, which was already crowded with kids throwing popcorn and making lots of noise. "No," she said. "We want to sit right up front."

The usher led them down the red-carpeted aisle. "In there," he said, waving his flashlight toward two empty seats.

The girls sat down just as the lights dimmed and a cartoon began.

"Amy, do you think I could ever come over to your house?" Jeannie whispered. "To Marianna's house, I mean."

"I don't know," Amy whispered back. "I'd have to ask my mother. Miss Morgan may not want us to have guests over."

"I'm sure it would be all right, if we stayed really quiet," Jeannie said.

"I'll ask my mother tomorrow," Amy said.

"Really?" Jeannie squealed. "Oooh, that would be swell!"

"Shhh!" said an angry voice behind her. "We want to hear the movie."

Jeannie and Amy slid down in their seats as a newsreel came on. It was called *Inside Nazi Germany*. Jeannie crunched on her Lifesavers as she watched long rows of German soldiers, marching past Adolf Hitler, the German dictator. Hitler saluted them with an outstretched arm as they passed. The next scene showed a group of British school-children being sent away from London on a train. They were going to the countryside, where they would be safe from German bombs. Many of the children and their mothers were crying.

At least we're safe here in California, Jeannie thought. Hitler would never come all the way to the United States.

She couldn't wait for *Fascinating Lady* to start, so she could forget all about the nasty old Germans. Barbara Cooper was much more interesting and glamorous. And all those soldiers were very far away.

CHAPTER TWO
"Amy Is an American Citizen"

The next morning, Jeannie was just finishing her corn flakes when the telephone rang. "It's for you, Jeannie," her mother called. "I think it's your friend Amy."

Jeannie jumped up from the table and took the receiver from her mother. "Hi, Amy," she said.

"Good news," Amy told her. "My mom says you can come over. Miss Morgan gave her permission."

"That's wonderful!" Jeannie cried.

"What's so wonderful?" her father asked grumpily from behind his newspaper.

Jeannie hung up the phone and began to dance around the kitchen. "Miss Morgan said yes!" she sang. "I'm going to a real movie star's house for the whole afternoon!"

"Now wait just a minute," Mr. Bosold said. "Exactly who is this Miss Morgan?"

"It's Marianna Morgan, the actress," Mrs. Bosold told him. "I'm sure you've heard of her, dear. Jeannie's little friend lives at her house, because Mrs. Mochida works there."

"Mochida?" Mr. Bosold frowned. "She's not one of those Japs, is she?"

Jeannie froze in mid-twirl. "Amy is an American citizen, just like us."

"She's Japanese first," Mr. Bosold said. "And don't you forget it."

"Bill!" Mrs. Bosold said, sounding shocked. "Amy is a lovely girl, and so is her mother. I met Mrs. Mochida at a PTA meeting. She's a very talented seamstress, and she made all the costumes for the school play. She's quite a hard worker, I must say."

"That's the problem with all the Japanese who have been flooding into this state," Mr. Bosold complained. "They work too hard. Believe me, they're after American jobs, and it's not just me who thinks so. You can ask any of the boys who work with me down at the aircraft plant. The Japs are taking over California, and the whole West Coast. Mark my words, those people will take over the world someday."

Jeannie's eyes filled with tears. How could her own father say such terrible things?

"That's enough, Bill," said Mrs. Bosold sharply. "Can't you see that you're upsetting Jeannie with your ridiculous talk? You seem to forget that your own family came to America from another country, too. Germany, in fact. How would you like someone to judge you the way you're judging the Mochidas?"

Mr. Bosold's face got very red. Then he cleared his throat and said to Mrs. Bosold, "I guess you're right, Eileen. I never thought of it that way.

"Go get dressed, Princess," he said to Jeannie a moment later. "I'll take you over to that Morgan woman's house."

"Thanks, Daddy," Jeannie said. She put her father's words out of her mind and ran down the hall to her bedroom.

She was going to have to wear something extra special. If she was really, really lucky, maybe some important director or agent would spot her and make her into a child star, like Judy Garland. She'd read about people being discovered like that.

Jeannie threw open her closet door and examined the contents. Most of her dresses looked alike. They had full skirts, round Peter Pan collars, and short, puffed sleeves. Jeannie chose her favorite blue plaid dress, white ankle socks, and her blue school shoes. Then she brushed her hair one hundred strokes, just the way the beauty magazines said girls should, and tied a blue ribbon on one side.

Not exactly star material, Jeannie thought as she gazed into the mirror. I look so—childish, she thought. Maybe what I need is some lipstick.

She was halfway to her parents' room when she decided against sneaking the tube of red lipstick from her mother's vanity table. She didn't want Amy to think she was getting too dressed up.

Her father was waiting outside in the family's shiny green Buick. "Now don't forget your manners," Mrs. Bosold warned, as Jeannie bounded out the door. "And don't bother Miss Morgan with too many questions."

"Don't worry, Mother," Jeannie said cheerfully, giving her a wave. "I'll be on my very best behavior. This is going to be one of the most exciting days in my whole life."

It took a while for Jeannie and her father

to find Marianna Morgan's house. It was a fancy peach stucco building with a red-tiled roof, located on the edge of one of the most fashionable areas in Hollywood. The house was set back from the street with a long, pebbled drive.

"I'll drive you to the door," Mr. Bosold said.

Jeannie was beginning to feel a little nervous now. What on earth was she going to say to Marianna Morgan?

But, of course, Miss Morgan didn't answer the door. Instead, a maid did. She was wearing a black dress, a frilly white apron, and a cap, just like in the movies. "Go around back," the woman told Jeannie. "Amy is out by the pool."

Jeannie waved good-bye to her father and made her way along the stone path at the side of the house. Sure enough, Amy was lying on a striped lounge chair, right next to a sparkling blue pool.

"Jeannie!" Amy called, jumping up. "I

thought you'd never get here."

"Neither did I," Jeannie answered. She looked around at the large gardens and the perfect green grass. "This is just beautiful, Amy."

Amy nodded. "Mr. Mura, the gardener, makes sure that the grounds always look perfect. See, he's working over there by the rosebushes."

Jeannie looked in the direction her friend was pointing. Sure enough, she saw an elderly Japanese man pruning some straggly branches covered with peach-colored rosebuds. Behind him was a teenage boy, who was also Japanese. They seemed to be arguing about something. The boy was waving his arms.

Amy shook her head. "Those two are at it again," she said. "They never get along."

"Who is the boy?" Jeannie asked.

"Oh, that's just Tadashi, Mr. Mura's grandson. He calls himself Tad for short, the way I call myself Amy instead of my real Japanese name, Emiko. Tad is *nisei*, just like me. That means we were born here in America. My mother and Mr. Mura are called *issei*, because they were born in Japan."

"So what do Tad and his grandfather argue about?" Jeannie asked as she and Amy headed toward the house.

Amy shrugged. "Oh, lots of things. Mr. Mura never raises his voice, but I can tell when he is angry. He thinks Tad is turning his back on his Japanese heritage. Tad says that he is American, and he rejects the old ways. That makes Mr. Mura very sad. He says that Tad has no respect for his elders."

Amy led Jeannie into the house through the servants' entrance, and Jeannie stared in awe at the huge tiled kitchen. There were sparkling new appliances along one wall and gleaming copper pans hanging above the stove. "This is bigger than my whole house," she said.

Amy laughed. "Wait till you see the living

room," she said. "And there's a ballroom, too."

"Where is Marianna?" Jeannie asked as they walked down a long, carpeted hallway. To her left, she could see an elaborate staircase, and to her right, a room with a white carpet and couches and a white baby grand piano.

"Oh, Miss Morgan is upstairs," Amy answered. "My mother is fitting her for some new gowns. We'll have to be very careful not to disturb them."

Suddenly, there was a loud bang from the front hall, and a man's voice called loudly, "Marianna! Where in blazes are you? I need to talk to you immediately!"

"It's Mr. Whick, the studio manager," Amy whispered. "Come on, we'd better get upstairs fast."

"What's the matter?" Jeannie asked, following her friend.

"I just don't want to see him, that's all," Amy said.

But it was too late.

"You there on the stairs, where is Miss Morgan?" the voice demanded.

Jeannie turned to see a short, perspiring man with a very red face and greased-back hair staring up at them.

"Miss Morgan is in her dressing room," Amy told him. "She said she didn't want to be disturbed."

"Get out of my way, you little brat," Mr. Whick said, taking the stairs two at a time. "I don't care what that woman told you. She'll make time to talk to me. Gem Studios owns her time."

"Yes, sir," Amy said meekly.

Jeannie watched the man disappear down the upstairs hallway. "What a grouch," she said. "I sure wouldn't want him as my manager if I was as famous as Marianna."

Amy sighed. "Mr. Whick's brother owns Gem Studios," she said. "That's how he got to be her manager. Besides, actors and actresses can't complain. If they make the men at the studio just a tiny bit angry, they can find themselves out of work for a long, long time—maybe even forever. Their own studio won't put them in any pictures, and none of the other studios will hire them, either."

"Well, that Mr. Whick is pretty awful," Jeannie said. "He looks a little like Hitler, don't you think?"

"You're right," Amy said, giggling. Then she looked serious again. "You know," she said in a low voice, "sometimes I think Mr. Whick doesn't like me because my family is Japanese."

Jeannie shook her head. "Don't be silly, Amy. That Mr. Whick is the kind of man who gets sore at everybody. I can just tell. And if I ever get to be a movie star, I won't have a mean old manager like him."

But deep down, Jeannie couldn't help remembering what her father had said about Japanese people that morning. If her own father felt that way, maybe Mr. Whick did, too.

CHAPTER THREE
"It's Like a Huge City in Here"

Jeannie was back at Marianna Morgan's house a few weeks later. It was Saturday afternoon, and she and Amy were supposed to be doing homework.

Instead, Jeannie was sitting cross-legged on Amy's bed, flipping through Amy's movie-star scrapbook. Amy was painting her nails bright red at a desk by the window.

Jeannie looked up from the scrapbook. "Will your mother let you wear that polish out of the house?" she asked.

"Of course not," Amy replied. "She'd probably kill me. I'll take it all off in a few minutes. I just wanted to see what it looked like."

Jeannie sighed and closed the scrapbook. "I'd love to get Lana Turner's autograph," she said.

"I'd rather have Clark Gable's," Amy said.

"Do you think you could get Marianna's autograph for me?" Jeannie asked. "I still haven't met her, you know."

"Well, she's on the set today," Amy said. She blew on her nails to dry them. "They're filming that new movie about a Southern woman who falls in love with a Northern soldier during the Civil War. It's a little bit like *Gone With the Wind*, I think."

"I loved that movie," Jeannie said dreamily. "I saw it six times."

Just then, the bedroom door opened, and Mrs. Mochida burst in. Her arms were full of colorful dresses. She almost dropped them when she saw Amy's nails.

"Mah, Emi Chan!" she said in horror. "What are you doing with that red paint? It's not for young girls!"

"I'm sorry, Mama," Amy said quickly. "I was going to take it right off."

But Amy's mother didn't seem to be listening. "I must get down to the studio right away," she said. "They need these dresses on the set."

"Oh, Mama, can we go with you?" Amy asked.

"No, Emiko, the director would never allow children on the set."

"Could we just ride to the studio with you?" Amy pleaded. "No one will even know we're there."

Jeannie held her breath. She was sure Mrs. Mochida would say no. But Amy's mother just sighed and said, "I suppose it wouldn't do any harm if you girls went along."

"It's Like a Huge City in Here"

Jeannie clapped her hands and bounced off the bed. "We're going to Gem Studios!" she cried, running over to give Amy a hug. The two of them danced around the carpet.

"I will go and get Mr. Ino," Mrs. Mochida said, hurrying from the room with the costumes.

"Who's Mr. Ino?" Jeannie asked Amy.

Amy grinned. "Miss Morgan's driver, of course. We're going in style!"

Jeannie couldn't believe she was getting to ride in a real limousine. The enormous, shiny black car had the longest nose she had ever seen.

All the way to the studio, Mrs. Mochida seemed very nervous. "I hope I'm not too late with these dresses," she kept saying.

Mr. Ino turned the car down Hollywood Boulevard. Finally, they reached the tall black iron gates of Gem Studios. The guard station behind it was painted with a big gold diamond, the studio's symbol.

"We're going to Set 5B, *The Prettiest Rebel in Dixie*," Mr. Ino told the man with the gold diamond stitched on his uniform.

The guard nodded and waved them in. Jeannie pressed her face against the window to see better.

Inside the gates were row after row of large white buildings. Each of them had a number on the side. Mr. Ino pulled the car up to number 5B.

Amy's mother scooped up Miss Morgan's dresses from the back seat. "I'll be back in a little while, girls," she said. "You wait right here in the car with Mr. Ino."

"There are so many people running around," Jeannie said, when Mrs. Mochida had gone into the building. "It's like a huge city in here."

"Except all the people are wearing costumes," Amy said. "Look at those cowboys and Indians over there."

"And there's a whole bunch of camels

going into Building 3A," Jeannie said, giggling. "Those ladies in the veils and funny pants are having a hard time getting past them."

There was a sudden knock on the car window, and the girls turned to see a fierce-looking pirate grinning at them. He had black teeth and a long scar on his cheek. Jeannie squealed and Amy quickly covered her eyes.

"It's okay. He's gone," Jeannie told her a few moments later.

"Good," Amy said, frowning. "I sure wouldn't want to run into him in the dark!"

Jeannie looked over at Mr. Ino. He was fast asleep in the front seat. His chauffeur's cap was tipped down over his face to block out the glare of the sun.

"Amy," Jeannie whispered. "Let's get out and take a look around."

Amy stared at her. "Are you crazy? Do you know how much trouble we'd get into if we got caught? What if Mr. Ino wakes up, or my mother comes back early and finds us gone?"

"Come on, Amy," Jeannie said. "This is the chance of a lifetime to see the Gem Studios lot. We might even get to watch Marianna on the set."

"We can't do that," Amy said. "Miss Morgan or my mother would spot us for sure."

Just then, Jeannie spied a group of women in long hooped skirts and large straw hats leaving the building marked 5B. "That's definitely the *Prettiest Rebel* set," she said. "Let's go."

Before her friend could protest, Jeannie dragged Amy out of the car and up to the big white building. No one seemed to notice them outside the door.

As soon as another group of actresses came out, chatting with a handsome bearded actor wearing a blue coat with gold buttons, Jeannie sneaked into the building. Amy was right behind her.

"It's Like a Huge City in Here"

They found themselves in an enormous, dark space. At one end, Jeannie could make out what looked like an old-fashioned drawing room. In front of it, men were operating cameras set on tall, three-legged stands. Next to the drawing room was another room with a frilly canopy bed. And beyond the bedroom was a quiet country lane that led nowhere.

"I wonder where Miss Morgan is," Amy whispered. "There are a bunch of ladies in the drawing room, but none of them looks like her."

"Cut!" a loud voice boomed, and an important-looking man with a megaphone walked onto the drawing room set.

"That must be the director," Jeannie said. "He seems to be in charge of everything."

"There's no sense in going through this scene again without Marianna," the man said. "She's still in Wardrobe. Take five, everybody. Joe, come take a look at these lights. We may have a problem here."

There was a great deal of commotion as the room suddenly came to life. People seemed to appear from nowhere, carrying lights on long poles and adjusting microphones.

The director seemed very upset about something as he talked to the man named Joe. As everyone bustled around them, Joe kept pointing up at the lights. Finally, the director picked up his megaphone and said, "Forget it, everybody. The lights are down. We'll break for lunch."

Gradually, all of the people in the room drifted away, and the director stalked off.

"I'm going up on one of those sets," Jeannie said.

"No, Jeannie, let's go back to the car," Amy pleaded. "My mother will have Miss Morgan's dresses pinned soon."

"Just for a minute, I promise," Jeannie said. She stared at the fake drawing room with its orange, crumpled-paper fireplace. It looked almost real.

She hurried toward it and sat down on a red velvet couch with gold fringe.

"Jeannie!" Amy called, glancing around. "We've got to get out of here."

"Oh, okay," Jeannie said reluctantly. Amy was right. There was no sense in pushing their luck.

But as she was getting up from the couch, she saw a large straw hat with a bright pink ribbon lying on the floor. Beside it was a beautiful painted fan.

"Hey, look at these," Jeannie called, picking them up. She placed the hat at a jaunty angle on her head. Then she held the fan just below her face. "Fiddle dee dee," she said, pretending she was Vivien Leigh, the actress who played Scarlett O'Hara in *Gone With the Wind*. "How do I look?"

"Gorgeous," Amy said with a grin. "Could I have your autograph, Miss Bosold?"

Jeannie lowered the fan and sighed. "I'll

have to change my name if I'm going to be a movie star," she said. "Bosold isn't very glamorous."

Suddenly a voice thundered, "Hey, you kids! What do you think you're doing?"

Jeannie's heart dropped. It was Mr. Whick, Miss Morgan's nasty manager! Immediately, she and Amy ran for the nearest exit.

"Do you think he recognized us?" Jeannie asked as they rushed through the door and onto the lot. Both of them were panting hard.

"I sure hope not," Amy said with a shudder, "or my mother and I will be packing our bags. Mr. Whick would use any excuse to get us out of Miss Morgan's house, I just know it."

CHAPTER FOUR
"Hey, Look, It's the Enemy"

At school on Monday, right after everyone had said the Pledge of Allegiance and sung "My Country, 'Tis of Thee," Jeannie felt a tap on the shoulder.

"I have something really exciting to tell you!" Amy said.

"What?" Jeannie asked eagerly.

"Amy Mochida and Jeannie Bosold, quiet, please," Miss Gleason said, frowning.

"I'll tell you at lunch," Amy whispered

quickly as they sat down.

It was a long way until noon. Bored, Jeannie ran her fountain pen around the inkwell on her desk as Miss Gleason droned on and on about the war in Europe again.

The teacher was explaining that the United States was still a neutral country. That meant that it had not officially taken sides in the war in Europe. The United States had also stayed neutral when Japan took control of China and started moving deeper into Asia.

"But even though we are not actually fighting, we can let the bully nations know that we do not approve of their actions," the teacher went on. "For instance, we can hurt Germany and Italy by selling or lending ships, planes, and guns to their enemies, England and France. And in the case of Japan, we could cut off their oil supply. Oil is something that armies need very badly for fuel, and the Japanese cannot get enough oil from their own land."

"Hey, Look, It's the Enemy"

Jeannie turned to sneak a look at Amy. Her friend was staring down at her desk. Poor Amy, Jeannie thought. After all, she was Japanese.

No, Jeannie corrected herself quickly. Amy was American, just like her. But Amy was also a—what was the word Amy had used?— *nisei*, a person who had been born in America but had Japanese parents. Most of the kids in the class, Jeannie knew, thought Amy was Japanese because she looked Japanese.

When the bell finally rang, the whole class rushed toward the door.

"Hey, look, it's the enemy!" Bud Peters said loudly as everyone headed toward the lunchroom. He was pointing right at Amy.

"Yeah, I bet she's a spy," Bud's friend Larry Turner added.

Amy bit her lip, but Jeannie whirled around angrily. "Shut up, you two," she said. "If you don't, I swear I'll…"

"Jeannie, please." Amy put a hand on

Jeannie's arm.

"They can't get away with saying stuff like that," Jeannie said, frowning. Why didn't Amy want to fight back? It wasn't her friend's fault that people who looked like her were going around taking over other countries. And no one in the class teased Vinnie D'Annuncio or Eric Dichter about being enemies, even though their parents had come from Italy and Germany.

When they reached the lunchroom, Jeannie and Amy sat down at an empty table and opened their brown paper bags. Jeannie had a bologna sandwich on white bread. Amy had some fancy chicken that was left over from one of Marianna Morgan's dinner parties.

"So, do you want to hear my big news?" Amy asked. She seemed determined to ignore the boys' hurtful remarks.

"Sure," Jeannie said, biting into her sandwich. Actually, she'd forgotten all about Amy having exciting news to tell her.

Amy's dark eyes were shining. "Well, Miss Morgan is having a very big party on Saturday night. It's kind of an early Christmas party, since she'll be going on a publicity tour for the first few weeks of December."

Jeannie stopped chewing. "Don't tell me. You're going to get to help at the party!"

"That's right," Amy said. "And so are you! My mom said you and I could watch the ladies' coats. We'll have to stay upstairs, but. . . "

"Yippee!" Jeannie cried, and the kids at the next table turned to stare at her. But she didn't care. She and Amy were going to spend a whole glittering evening watching famous movie stars! How was she ever going to wait until Saturday?

Sure enough, the rest of the week seemed to drag on endlessly. Finally, the big night arrived. At six o'clock sharp, Jeannie's father dropped her off and she walked up to Marianna Morgan's back doorstep and rang the bell.

Amy opened the door. "Come on in," she said with a big smile. "Merry Christmas, four weeks early."

"Merry Christmas to you, too," Jeannie replied, stepping inside.

Her mouth dropped open when she saw the piles of hors d'oeuvres laid out on shining silver trays with fancy white paper doilies. There were small, yummy-looking cheese pies, tiny hot dogs rolled in flaky biscuits, perfect pink shrimp, and stuffed mushrooms. The cook was taking a steaming dish out of the oven, and one of the maids was stirring a great bowl of eggnog.

"Watch out for the glasses," Amy warned as Jeannie followed her through the kitchen to the butler's pantry. The long counter was covered with trays of sparkling crystal in all sizes and shapes.

"I'll be careful, all right," Jeannie said, walking gingerly past the counter.

"I've already taken some treats upstairs for

us," Amy told her. "The guests won't be arriving for an hour or so."

Just as they reached the hallway, Jeannie saw a beautiful red-haired woman in a long, jade green dress hurrying down the grand staircase. It was Marianna Morgan herself!

"Hello there, Amy," said the actress as she spotted them. She had a throaty, breathless-sounding voice. Or maybe it was just because she'd been running, Jeannie thought.

"And you must be Jeannie," Miss Morgan added. "Mrs. Mochida told me you were coming to spend the night. How very nice for Amy to have a friend come and visit in this big old lonely house." She held out her hand. "I'm Marianna Morgan."

Jeannie nearly fainted. Marianna Morgan knew her name! "It's n-nice to meet you," she stammered. The actress's hand was very soft as Jeannie shook it. She probably used oodles of hand cream, like the movie stars in all the ads.

"Well, you girls enjoy yourselves," Miss

Morgan said. "I have to check in with my kitchen staff to make sure everything is ready. Bye now."

The actress hurried on her way, leaving behind a cloud of expensive French perfume.

"She's beautiful," Jeannie said in awe.

"And she's nice, too," Amy added, heading up the stairs. "It's too bad that Mr. Whick is always telling her what to do and say. I feel sorry for her sometimes."

The girls posted themselves in a lilac-colored bedroom near the stairs and waited for the guests to arrive. Mrs. Mochida was going to take the ladies' coats, but Amy and Jeannie would be in charge of hanging them up.

"So who do you think we'll get to meet?" Jeannie asked, as she reached for one of the tiny hot dogs that Amy had brought up.

"Probably lots of big stars," Amy said. "Even if they don't come to check on their coats, the ladies will want to freshen up in the powder room."

Two hours later, the bedroom was full of coats, but the girls still hadn't met a single movie star at the party.

"Maybe we could go down there for a little while," Jeannie said finally. "Just to the kitchen or something, I mean."

Amy shook her head. "I promised my mother we'd stay up here, remember? But I guess we could sit on the stairs and watch the party."

Jeannie grinned. "Let's go!"

Within moments, the girls were leaning over the balcony rail. Jeannie tried desperately to spot somebody famous.

"Look, there's Rita Hayworth!" Amy said. "Her hair's almost the same color as Miss Morgan's."

"And Joan Crawford's over by that potted plant, listening to someone play the piano," Jeannie added. "This must be the swellest party ever!"

"Do you think Clark Gable's down there

somewhere?" Amy asked wistfully. "I'm sure Miss Morgan invited him. Maybe I could pretend to be serving hors d'oeuvres and slip him a cocktail napkin to sign for my movie star scrapbook. Or maybe…"

"Shh!" Jeannie interrupted. "Don't look now, but Mr. Hitler-Whick is right below us. He's talking to a bunch of men who look just like him. They've all got patent-leather hair."

She strained her ears to hear the men's conversation.

"It's a shame we aren't doing more to help the Allies," one of them was saying.

"We'll be in the war in Europe soon enough," another man said.

A third man flicked his cigar on the carpet. "Well, Hollywood has been doing its part to prepare this country for action," he said. "What about the *March of Time* series we've been showing in the theaters for the last six years? Twenty-minute films, one every month. Take *Inside Nazi Germany*, for instance. It got people stirred up, all right. Why, our boys were just itching to get over there and pound those Nazis."

"And there have been plenty of full-length films made about the war, too," the second man put in. "All designed to put people's sympathies in the right place. *Confessions of a Nazi Spy, Foreign Correspondent, Escape*—more films than I can count. A lot of our stars come from Europe, and so do most of the studio owners. Believe me, they're happy to fight Hitler in their own way."

Mr. Whick smiled. "That's all well and good, gentlemen," he said. "But don't forget the best part. Once America has jumped into the war, the people left at home will be lining up at the box office. They'll want to escape all of their problems, forget that their loved ones are fighting overseas. We'll throw a few handsome soldiers up on the screen, a few tearful blonde sweethearts. The money will be rolling in all over Hollywood!"

Just then, Mrs. Mochida came up to the men and offered them a tray of hors d'oeuvres.

"You know what I think, gentlemen?" Mr. Whick said, as soon as Amy's mother turned away. "I think we're all missing the real enemy we need to fight. Hitler is small potatoes." He nodded toward Mrs. Mochida, who had moved on to the next group of guests. "The biggest threat to the world is right in this room—the Japs."

Jeannie drew back in horror and glanced over at Amy. Her friend didn't seem to have heard. She was busy watching Veronica Lake dance with Humphrey Bogart.

That Mr. Whick is an awful man, Jeannie thought. America is never going to go to war—with anybody.

CHAPTER FIVE
"I Guess I Feel More American than Japanese"

The next Saturday afternoon, Jeannie and Amy went all the way to the other side of Los Angeles by streetcar, transferring several times from one streetcar line to another. Amy was going to Little Tokyo to visit her Grandmother Mochida, and she had invited Jeannie to go with her.

As the streetcar approached their stop, Jeannie twisted and untwisted her hands in her lap. The whole way, she had worried that her parents would find out that she had gone across town to a strange place. They thought she and Amy were at the movies.

Mrs. Mochida hadn't been crazy about the idea of the girls going to Little Tokyo alone, either, especially with all the transfers they had to make. That's why she had asked Tad, Mr. Mura's grandson, to go with them. Jeannie didn't see why Tad had to be their big protector. He was only a few years older than she and Amy. And he had talked nonstop about baseball ever since they'd left Hollywood.

Amy looked anxiously out the window as the other passengers got up from their seats. "I hope we can find Oba San's apartment," she said. "I haven't been to Little Tokyo in a long time, and my mother always goes with me."

"Don't worry, we'll find the place," Tad said. "We can always ask someone if we get lost."

"I Guess I Feel More American than Japanese"

Jeannie wasn't so sure about asking for directions when they stepped off the streetcar. It seemed as though they had just entered a foreign country, right in the middle of California.

Little Tokyo was very crowded. It was noisy, too. Jeannie stared down the narrow streets of tiny shops and laundries and restaurants. All around her, men, women, and children were speaking Japanese. A few feet away, a woman was arguing with an old man, probably over the price of the vegetables he was selling. Behind the man were cages full of squawking chickens.

"Can you understand what everyone is saying?" Jeannie asked Amy.

Amy shook her head. "Not very well," she said. "My mother keeps trying to teach me Japanese, but it's so hard to learn."

"These people should all learn English," Tad said. "They're in America now. How will anyone ever see us as real Americans if we keep holding onto the old ways?"

"Well, not all of these people are Americans," Amy pointed out. "Many of them were born in Japan. The American government won't allow Asian-born people to become citizens, remember?"

Jeannie frowned. "Why not?" she asked. "People from other countries can become Americans after a few years."

"Beats me," Tad said with a shrug. "Becoming a citizen is part of the American dream."

Amy reached into the pocket of her red plaid dress and took out a small piece of notebook paper. "My mother drew us a map," she said. "It looks like Oba San lives about six blocks east and three blocks south from where the streetcar let us off."

Jeannie, Amy, and Tad wandered through the narrow, busy streets until they found Grandmother Mochida's house. It was a tiny apartment above a shop. Jeannie couldn't read the sign in the shop's window, but she could see several young Japanese girls working at sewing machines in the back.

Grandmother Mochida seemed very glad to see them. She was a short, plump woman with gray hair pulled into a bun. Her face was full of wrinkles, but she smiled at them warmly. She was wearing a brightly colored cotton kimono.

Amy and Tad both bowed to the older woman as a sign of respect. Jeannie bowed, too.

Grandmother Mochida waved them in. Jeannie saw Amy and Tad remove their shoes just outside the door, so she took her shoes off as well.

The apartment had only two rooms, and there wasn't very much furniture. In a far corner, partially hidden by a screen, Jeannie noticed a woven straw mat covered with a white quilt. That was probably where Amy's grandmother slept. On a small black table in the main room she saw a candle burning next to a framed photograph of an elderly Japanese man.

"That's my grandfather," Amy whispered beside her. "Oba San honors his spirit. He died back in Japan, before I was born."

The girls and Tad followed the tiny woman to a long, low table. Then she said something in Japanese. Amy and Tad smiled and kneeled down at the table.

"Sit down, Jeannie," Amy said, patting the floor beside her. "Oba San has been expecting us. We're going to have something to eat."

"Should we help bring the things out?" Jeannie asked in a low voice. At home, she always brought the plates and food to the table for her mother.

Amy shook her head. "No," she said. "Oba San will want to serve us herself."

Grandmother Mochida brought each of them a little black tray. First, they had bowls of steaming, clear soup with thick noodles.

Then came slices of some kind of black fish.

"It's eel," Amy told Jeannie.

"Eel?" Jeannie gulped. She had once seen the long, shiny, oily creatures at Fisherman's Wharf in San Francisco.

But Grandmother Mochida was smiling and nodding at her, and Jeannie didn't want to be rude. She smiled back and took a few tiny bites of the broiled eel, trying to forget how ugly they were when they were alive. It didn't taste as bad as she thought, but she was relieved when Amy's grandmother brought out rice and slivered cucumbers.

There wasn't much conversation at the little table, but no one seemed to mind. It was a very cozy apartment, and by the time the four of them had hot green tea and little sweet cakes, Jeannie was feeling very much at home.

"These are delicious," she told Grandmother Mochida, pointing to the plate of cakes.

"They're bean paste," Tad told her with a

grin. "Not exactly chocolate chip, huh?"

Amy frowned at him, but Jeannie took a third cake that Grandmother Mochida offered her. "Thank you," she said. "I wish my mom knew how to make these."

Soon, it was almost five o'clock, and Jeannie, Amy, and Tad said good-bye to Grandmother Mochida.

When they stepped outside again, the streets were still crowded. Women were rushing to buy last-minute items for dinner, and children were chattering and playing on the corners. Some shopkeepers were locking their stores for the night.

Jeannie saw one restaurant that was filled with Japanese men of all ages. "That place must have really good food," she said.

"That's a teahouse," Amy told her. "The men go there to meet and talk. Sometimes they stay for hours. It's like a club."

"This was a lot of fun," Jeannie said. "I wish we didn't have to go home so soon.

Little Tokyo is such an interesting place."

"It is interesting," Amy agreed. "But sometimes I feel very funny here. I guess I really feel more American than Japanese."

"Well, you are American," Tad said. "And if you don't live here in Little Tokyo, and you don't speak the language, what do you expect?"

"I'm not really sure," Amy said slowly. "I mean, you and I look Japanese, right? Japanese people and American people all think we're Japanese rather than American. Did you see how strangely that old Japanese woman back there looked at me when I had to tell her I couldn't read that street sign?"

"Maybe," Tad said, shrugging. "But I sure will be glad to get back to Hollywood. As soon as we get home, I'm going to stop at the drugstore and get a black and white soda."

"You and your food," Amy said with a sniff. "Is that all you think about, besides baseball?"

"Well, I'd rather have an ice cream soda than drink green tea," Tad retorted. "I'll take American food any day."

"You can't tell me that Japanese traditions aren't important to you," Amy said, putting her hands on her hips.

"You take things too seriously, Amy," Tad replied. "I'm not knocking Japanese things. But you know how I feel about the old ways. My grandfather and I argue all the time about the way I should live my life. My grandfather says I have no respect for my ancestors and our traditions. That's not true. But I am American, and I need to follow American traditions, too."

Jeannie didn't want Tad and Amy to argue. "Look, it's getting really late," she said, pointing to a display of watches in a nearby shop. "If we don't hurry, we'll miss the next streetcar."

The three of them made it to the corner just in time to hop on the streetcar before it left. On the way home, both Amy and Tad were very quiet. Then Tad leaned over the seat behind them and tapped Amy on the shoulder.

"I want you to know something, Amy Mochida," he said. "If this country ever goes to war, I'm going to enlist. Then I'll prove to everyone that I'm a real American."

Amy frowned. "Stop it, Tad," she said. "You're too young to be a soldier."

"That's right," Jeannie said, turning around. "And besides, there isn't going to be any war."

Tad slumped back in his seat. "What do you know?" he said. "You're just girls, anyway."

Jeannie was about to give Tad a piece of her mind, but she bit her tongue when she saw Amy's face. Her friend looked so upset.

Why did everyone keep insisting there was going to be a war?

CHAPTER SIX
"This Means War"

When they arrived back in Hollywood, Jeannie got off the streetcar with Amy and Tad. She wanted to call her mother to see if Amy could spend the night.

It was very quiet at Marianna Morgan's house. The actress was on a publicity tour for a new film, and no one expected her back for two months. Some of the servants had gone home to visit their families, but a few had remained to keep the house running smoothly. Mrs. Mochida was working on some new dresses that would be shipped to Miss Morgan on tour.

Jeannie called her mother from the darkened kitchen. Amy was welcome to stay with them for the rest of the weekend!

Jeannie hung up the phone, feeling relieved. She had been a tiny bit worried that her father might say no. She knew he still didn't want her to be such good friends with Amy. But now it looked as though her father might finally be changing his mind about all that. Thank heavens, Jeannie thought.

Mr. Bosold picked the girls up, and they all had dinner as soon as they arrived back at Jeannie's house. Jeannie was still a little full from all the food they'd had at Grandmother Mochida's, but as far as her parents knew, she and Amy had been at the movies all afternoon. Jeannie ate every bit of pot roast, praying that Amy wouldn't slip up and mention Little Tokyo or visiting her grandmother.

Luckily, her secret was still safe when dinner was over. Jeannie and Amy got into their pajamas and everyone listened to the radio in the living room. It was a comedy hour, and no one laughed louder than Amy.

Good, Jeannie thought. She's happy again.

The girls made popcorn and drank Cokes and stayed up very late. They did each other's hair in the latest styles, looked at Jeannie's movie star magazines, and talked about the boys in their class. Finally, Jeannie's mother knocked on the door and told them it was time to go to sleep.

In the morning, Jeannie went to church with her parents. She knew that Amy always went to church on Sundays, too, but Amy had announced at breakfast that she had a bit of a stomach ache. Jeannie wondered whether Amy was just feeling uncomfortable about going to church with someone else's family, but she didn't say anything.

By the time they returned home for lunch,

Amy seemed to have made a complete recovery. She helped Mrs. Bosold and Jeannie prepare the soup and sandwiches for lunch and set the table.

Just as Jeannie was walking back into the kitchen to get more napkins, she heard a loud pounding at the kitchen door.

Jeannie's mother heard the pounding, too. "Now who could that be?" she said, frowning. "Making so much noise on a Sunday afternoon." She quickly removed her apron and opened the door.

It was Mrs. Wright, who lived two houses down. Jeannie didn't like the sharp-nosed woman much, because she never minded her own business.

Mrs. Wright seemed very upset. "I saw your car pull in a few minutes ago," she said. "Have you heard the news?"

"Why, no," Jeannie's mother said. "What news?"

"Well, it's just the most terrible thing,"

Mrs. Wright said, wringing her hands. The flower on her black hat was bobbing up and down. "The naval base..." Suddenly, she stopped, and her mouth dropped open.

Jeannie thought Mrs. Wright was staring at her, until she realized that Amy was standing right behind her in the kitchen doorway. Maybe their nosy neighbor thought the Bosolds had a new Japanese daughter.

But Mrs. Wright's face just turned purple. "Why, Eileen Bosold, I never!" she sputtered. Then she whirled around and started quickly down the walk, her high heels clicking on the concrete.

"What on earth was all that about?" Jeannie's mother said, shaking her head as she closed the door. "That Mabel Wright is certainly a very strange woman."

"Maybe we should turn on the radio," Jeannie said.

"What's going on?" Mr. Bosold asked, coming into the kitchen in his slippers. He had *Life* magazine tucked under his arm.

"Mrs. Wright just came over to see if we had heard some kind of news," Jeannie told him. "She said something about a naval base, but then…"

Mr. Bosold immediately headed into the living room. "Let's turn on the radio, then," he said. "That sounds serious."

Looking nervous, Jeannie's mother followed him. Jeannie and Amy exchanged glances and went into the living room, too. Mr. Bosold turned on the radio and fiddled with the tuning for a moment.

An urgent voice cracked into the living room. Japan, the radio announcer said, had attacked the United States naval base and army air field at Pearl Harbor, Hawaii.

Mrs. Bosold's hand went to her throat. "That can't be true," she said. "It must be some kind of mistake."

"Quiet, Eileen," Mr. Bosold said. "Let's listen to the report. This will mean war."

Beside Jeannie, Amy burst into tears. Jeannie could tell that her friend was trying not to make any noise, but her shoulders were heaving, and she was taking in great gulps of air.

"It's okay, Amy," Jeannie said, trying to comfort her. She put her arms around her friend, and Amy buried her face in her shoulder. "It can't be true," Jeannie echoed her mother. "It's probably just some crazy person. Or a fake radio report, like that one where everyone thought the Earth was being invaded by Martians. You know, like 'War of the Worlds.'"

But her father was motioning to her to stop talking. The announcer was saying that they didn't have many details yet, but the naval base had been attacked at dawn. Many men were believed dead, and several ships and planes had been destroyed.

Then Mrs. Bosold got up and snapped off the radio. "That's enough for now," she said, ignoring her husband's furious look. "Why don't we all have our lunch? It's getting cold out there on the table."

"I-I don't think I can eat anything," Amy said, sniffling. "I think I should go home. I want to see my mother."

"Nonsense," Mrs. Bosold said. "If you're thinking that we don't want you here now, that's absolutely ridiculous."

Mr. Bosold stood up and cleared his throat. "Jeannie's mother is right that we'd like you to stay, Amy," he said. "But I'm afraid you may be right, too. If this news of a Japanese attack on the United States is true, you should get home right away. Even if the report is false, some people may be out looking for trouble. The sooner you're safe in your own home, the better. Your mother may be worried about you."

"Don't you think you're exaggerating the danger, dear?" Mrs. Bosold asked her husband anxiously. "After all, she's only a child."

But Mr. Bosold's face was grim. "Amy, go

up and pack your things. I'll take you to Miss Morgan's house right away."

"I'm coming, too," Jeannie spoke up.

"No, honey, I want you to stay here," Mrs. Bosold said. "If your father's right, and there is some kind of angry mob out there . . ." Her voice trailed away.

"But I'll be with Daddy," Jeannie objected. "We'll be safe. And Amy is my very best friend."

Jeannie's mother looked helplessly at Jeannie's father. "I'll take her," he said. "But we have to go now."

Amy reappeared, dragging her overnight case. Her eyes were red and puffy. "I'm ready," she said in a shaky voice.

No one said anything all the way to Marianna Morgan's house. Jeannie thought the streets looked unusually quiet. Everyone was probably gathered around their radios at home, waiting for another news report.

As soon as they pulled into Miss Morgan's

driveway, Mrs. Mochida came to the front door. Jeannie's father quickly stopped the car, and Amy jumped out. She gave her mother a big hug, and the two of them held onto each other for a moment.

"Stay here," Jeannie's father told her as he got out of the car and went around back to get Amy's suitcase.

Jeannie quickly rolled down the window. "Amy!" she called.

Amy ran back to the car. "Everyone's heard the report," she said. "And the attack was just confirmed on the radio. It must be true, Jeannie. I can't believe it!"

"Neither can I," Jeannie said. "But don't worry. All the fuss will die down soon. And even if we do go to war..."

"Jeannie, my mother and I have to leave Hollywood," Amy interrupted. "She just told me. Mr. Whick fired all of Miss Morgan's Japanese employees an hour ago."

"What!" Jeannie cried. "He can't do that!

What are you talking about?"

"It is all true," said Mrs. Mochida sadly, coming up behind Amy. "Mr. Whick told us that it would be unwise for Miss Morgan to be associated in any way with the enemy."

"The enemy?" Jeannie asked in disbelief. She started to get out of the car.

But her father put a firm hand on the door. "Mrs. Mochida, we are very sorry to hear about all of this," he said. Jeannie could tell that he really meant it. "Is there anything we can do?"

Amy's mother shook her head. "Thank you for your kindness," she said, with tears in her eyes. "But our bags are already packed. Amy and I will be going to Little Tokyo to stay with my mother-in-law. She may need us now. We are leaving tonight, with Mr. Mura and his grandson."

Mr. Bosold extended his hand. "I wish you the very best of luck," he said. "And again, please let us know if there is anything you need."

"This Means War"

"Thank you, Mr. Bosold. I am sure that Amy and I will be fine."

Jeannie couldn't believe she was hearing this. It was all so unfair! The minute her father let go of the car door, she hopped out and threw her arms around Amy. "Good-bye," she said, trying not to cry. "You'll write to me, won't you?"

"Of course I will," Amy said quietly. "I'll tell you about my new school and everything."

"I just know you'll be able to come back soon," Jeannie said. "Maybe I can even visit you in Little Tokyo." But even as she said that, she knew it wasn't true.

"Let's go, Jeannie," her father said. "The Mochidas have a lot to do, I'm sure."

Jeannie waved to Amy and Mrs. Mochida from the back of the car the whole way down the driveway. She had a feeling it was going to be a long time before she'd see her best friend again.

CHAPTER SEVEN
"She's Safer with Her Own People"

Weeks after Amy and her mother had left for Little Tokyo, Jeannie had still not heard from her friend. She knew that Grandmother Mochida didn't have a telephone, but surely Amy would have written to her by now. Jeannie was getting worried.

It had been a very quiet Christmas for everyone. At President Roosevelt's request, Congress had declared that the United States was now at war with Japan in the Pacific, and with Germany and Italy in Europe. Every day, more men were enlisting to fight, and families were being torn apart. But Americans were angry after the Japanese attack on Pearl Harbor, and eager for revenge. Until now, they had always felt that the United States was safe from attack by a foreign country.

Jeannie dreaded going to school and looking at Amy's empty desk. Miss Gleason had simply told the class that Amy and her family had moved out of town. On the playground, the boys played war games, running all over the place fighting "Japs." All the children had to wear identification tags around their necks. Several times a week, the bells would ring for air raid drills, and everyone had to sit in the corridors or under their desks. Every week, there seemed to be some kind of collection drive for the war effort. Kids began asking their parents and neighbors for old newspapers, string, and scrap metal. They felt very patriotic when they crushed tin cans with their feet and brought them to school. The students who collected the most won prizes.

One day after school, when Jeannie had again checked the mailbox and found no letter from Amy, she went straight to her room and started to cry.

"Jeannie?" her mother called through the door. "Honey, can I come in?"

Jeannie buried her face in her pillow. She wanted to be alone right now, but she didn't want to hurt her mother's feelings.

The door opened, and Jeannie's mother came in and sat down on the bed. "Please don't cry, darling," she said, stroking Jeannie's hair. "Your father and I hate to see our little princess so sad. How about if we all go to the movies together tonight? You'd like that, wouldn't you, sweetie?"

"No thanks," Jeannie said, her voice muffled. She hated going to the movies now. It reminded her of all the afternoons she'd spent downtown at the theater with Amy. Besides, she didn't want to see all the newsreels about the war.

Mrs. Bosold sighed. "Jeannie," she said, "I know you're very upset about Amy moving to Little Tokyo. You're probably angry, too. But believe me, honey, she's safer with her own people."

"We're her people," Jeannie said, sitting up. "I keep telling you, she's American."

"I know that," Mrs. Bosold said gently. "And you know that. But she looks Japanese. You know, Jeannie, there have already been some incidents in which Japanese-Americans have been seriously hurt. There are some angry people out there who hold any person in any way connected with Japan responsible for this war."

"I know," Jeannie sniffed. "But it just isn't fair. Amy and her mother never hurt anyone. And they're not spies, either."

"Well, Jeannie, you're right. It isn't fair. But you're going to have to get on with your life, just like Amy. I'm sure you'll hear from her sometime soon. She's probably going through a lot right now. She's living in a new house and going to a new school. I'm sure she hasn't forgotten you, dear, if that's what you're worried about."

Jeannie nodded. "I know. I guess I'm being selfish, aren't I?"

Mrs. Bosold leaned over and gave her a kiss on the forehead. "I don't think so, Jeannie. You're just a little worried, that's all. Now dry your tears and come on down to dinner."

After her mother had left, Jeannie crossed the hall to the bathroom and splashed cold water on her face. Her eyes still looked puffy, but she felt better. Maybe she'd just needed to cry a little. Besides, she had a plan.

She was going to get Mrs. Mochida's job back, no matter what it took. As soon as Marianna Morgan got back from her tour, she was going to beg the actress to rehire Amy's mother. Miss Morgan had seemed like a very nice lady. And she needed a good seamstress, too. It was worth a try.

A few weeks later, Jeannie finally found a letter from Amy in the mailbox. She was so excited that she tore the envelope open on the spot and dropped it to the floor as she yanked out the letter's lined pages.

Dear Jeannie,

I'm sorry it's taken so long for me to write. I've been trying very hard to get used to being in Little Tokyo. I like living with Grandmother Mochida, but it is very crowded with the three of us here. And I never get to go to the movies. We don't have any money, because Mama hasn't found a new job yet. None of the shopkeepers are hiring new people. Some of our neighbors are even talking about leaving California, but I don't think we will. We have nowhere to go, and

Grandmother Mochida would never leave Little Tokyo, anyway. I see Tad sometimes. He's in the junior high. The kids at my new school are okay, but I don't know any of them very well yet. Most of them speak Japanese at home, but their English is okay. Grandmother Mochida's address is on the envelope. I hope we can still be best friends.

Love,
Amy

P.S. Please write back soon.

Jeannie raced straight into the house and grabbed a pen and notebook paper from her schoolbag. Then she sat down to write back to Amy. It was hard to start because she wanted the letter to sound funny and cheerful. Jeannie decided not to say anything about her plan. She didn't want to get her friend's hopes up.

Over the next few days, Jeannie read every movie magazine she could get her hands on. She didn't have enough money to buy all of them, so she read them at the drugstore, which made Mr. Fitzwater, the owner, a little angry. But she had to find out when Marianna Morgan was returning home.

Finally, Jeannie found what she was looking for in the gossip column of *Modern Screen* magazine. Miss Morgan's tour had just ended. She was headed back to Hollywood!

Right after school the next afternoon, Jeannie took the streetcar to the actress's neighborhood. She had absolutely no idea what she would say to Miss Morgan. But she just had to try.

Jeannie got off the streetcar a few blocks from the house and started walking. A very long black limousine passed, and she thought it might be Miss Morgan's. The driver wasn't Mr. Ino, but Miss Morgan probably had a new chauffeur now. Mr. Ino was Japanese, so Mr. Whick had fired him, too.

Sure enough, the limousine pulled into Marianna Morgan's driveway. Jeannie quickened her steps. Maybe she could just catch the actress as she was getting out of the car.

But by the time Jeannie reached the driveway, Miss Morgan had already gone into the house. There was another limousine in the driveway, too.

Quickly, Jeannie made her way toward the house. She hid behind trees and bushes as she went, so that no one would see her until she had reached the front door.

Finally, Jeannie walked up the steps and boldly rang the bell. To her surprise, there was no answer. Maybe Miss Morgan didn't have a new maid yet.

Then she heard voices at the side of the house. Jeannie walked quietly down the flagstone path toward the pool. It seemed like ages since Amy had greeted her there.

The voices grew louder. Jeannie ducked behind a rosebush, but no one seemed to notice her. The voices belonged to Mr. Whick and Marianna Morgan.

"I won't have it, I tell you!" Marianna was saying. "How dare you fire my household staff behind my back!"

"Do remember, Marianna, that Gem Studios pays their salaries. And the studio is not going to finance a payroll full of enemy Japs. They were probably all spies, anyway.

"That's ridiculous!" Marianna said. "I'm going to have a talk with that brother of yours. I tell you, I won't have you sticking your nose in my affairs like this. I'm sick of it! This is the last straw."

"Go ahead and complain to anyone you want," Mr. Whick said. He sounded very angry, and his bald spot was all sweaty. "The studio will support me on this. And you'd better watch your step, Marianna. You'll be nothing without Gem Studios. You'll never work again."

"I don't care!" Marianna shouted, dismissing Mr. Whick with a wave of her hand. "If being a big star means listening to nasty little men like you for the rest of my life, then I'm through with Hollywood. Now get off my property!"

"Think about what you're saying, Marianna," Mr. Whick said, trying not to smile. "This isn't your property. It belongs to Gem Studios. Throw me out, and you're throwing away your whole career. You'll have nothing. You'll be nothing."

"Perhaps you are deaf, Mr. Whick," Marianna said through clenched teeth. "Or just plain stupid. I believe I told you to leave."

Jeannie's mouth dropped open as the short, scowling man stormed past her, heading for the driveway. He hadn't even seen her. And Marianna had plopped onto one of the lounge chairs.

This is it, Jeannie thought. It's now or never.

She stepped out from behind the rosebush and walked over to the actress's chair. Then she drew a deep breath.

"Um—Miss Morgan?"

The actress turned around. For a minute she looked as though she had heard a ghost. But then she saw Jeannie, and she seemed to relax.

"I'm sorry to bother you," Jeannie said, her words coming out in a rush. "And I didn't mean to eavesdrop. But I really had to talk to you, and…"

"You're Amy's little friend from school, aren't you? Jeannie Boswell?"

"Bosold," Jeannie said. "I'm here because I wanted to ask whether you'd consider giving Mrs. Mochida her job back. She and Amy don't know I'm doing this, but I thought…" Suddenly, Jeannie's mind went blank, and she wasn't sure what to say next. It was all happening so fast.

Marianna Morgan smiled. "That's very sweet of you, Jeannie Bosold. I'm sure Amy would appreciate what you're trying to do. But to tell you the truth, Jeannie, I'm not sure that I'll have a job to give Mrs. Mochida now. I may not have a job myself."

"Oh," Jeannie said, feeling stupid.

The actress rose from her chair. "I'll tell you what," she said. "If I keep my job, I'll give Mrs. Mochida hers back, too. If she wants it, that is."

Jeannie nodded. "Oh, thank you so much, Miss Morgan. I'm sure she will." But deep down, she suddenly wasn't sure. Maybe Amy's mother wouldn't want to come back to Hollywood now. Maybe Grandmother Mochida needed her more than Marianna Morgan did. Maybe she'd be afraid to return to a place where Japanese people were seen as enemies.

"I have something for Amy," Miss Morgan said. "Would you give it to her for me? It's just a little thing, and I'm not sure where she is right now."

"I'll take it to her," Jeannie said.

"Wait here," the actress said. She went

into the house and came out a few minutes later, carrying something in her hand. Jeannie saw that it was a glossy photograph.

"Amy always wanted this," Marianna said. "Clark and I were on tour together."

Jeannie stared at the photograph. In the bottom right-hand corner, the actor had written, "To Amy, with all my love. Clark Gable."

"Wow!" Jeannie exclaimed, taking the photograph from Miss Morgan very carefully. "She'll be so excited."

Marianna Morgan nodded. "Well, you can tell her mother what I said about the job. Have her call me in a few weeks or so. Good-bye now."

"Good-bye," Jeannie said, feeling a little dazed. Miss Morgan was already heading back into the house. "Thanks again!" she called. She couldn't wait to find Amy now! She was so full of expectation she could hardly stand it. Amy would be so pleased.

CHAPTER 8
"We're Going to Be Prisoners of War"

The next day at school, Jeannie hardly heard a word Miss Gleason said. All she could think about was how she was going to Little Tokyo the minute the last bell rang.

She had it all planned. She'd take the streetcar to Hollywood Boulevard, then transfer to another streetcar line, and later to a third line that would take her to Little Tokyo, just the way she and Amy and Tad had done last December. Hopefully, it wouldn't be too hard to find Grandmother Mochida's house. Jeannie could hardly wait to see the look on her best friend's face when she opened the door!

Jeannie was glad she hadn't tried to visit Amy sooner. True, she had been tempted to go to Little Tokyo before, once or twice. But now she would have a special present for Amy—and some very good news about her mother's job! Jeannie felt sure that Marianna Morgan wouldn't be fired by Gem Studios. After all, she was going to be a really big star. She was already a pretty big star. Why would the studio let all the money they had spent on her go down the drain?

Jeannie's plan went like clockwork. She made the right streetcar connection and each time sat right up front behind the motorman. As soon as they reached Little Tokyo, Jeannie was the first one off the streetcar. The sooner she reached the Mochida's house, the more time she'd get to spend with Amy.

But as Jeannie started off in the direction she was sure Grandmother Mochida lived, something didn't feel right.

What was it Amy had said when she looked at that map her mother had given her? Six blocks east, three blocks south? Now Jeannie wasn't sure. The streets looked vaguely familiar, but definitely not the same.

Then Jeannie realized what was wrong. The streets weren't crowded this time. A few shops were open, but most of them were boarded up. Others had "For Sale" or "For Rent" signs in the window. Where had all the people gone? Jeannie began to feel as though she were walking through a ghost town.

Finally, Jeannie came to Grandmother Mochida's street. She recognized the sign outside the shop below her apartment. But when she reached the shop, she saw that it was empty. All of the sewing machines had disappeared.

Her heart pounding, Jeannie rang the bell to the Mochidas' apartment. Was she too late? What if Amy and her family had left, too? Where would they have gone? And how would she ever find Amy again?

To Jeannie's relief, Amy opened the door. Her friend's round face broke into a happy smile. "Jeannie!" she cried. "Am I glad to see you!"

"Who is it, Amy?" Mrs. Mochida called.

"It's Jeannie, Mama. She's come to say good-bye."

Good-bye? Jeannie was puzzled. She'd just arrived!

"Come in, come in," Amy's mother said, appearing at the door.

Jeannie took off her shoes and stepped inside. The whole apartment looked different, too.

Grandmother Mochida was sitting in a chair in the corner. She smiled sadly at Jeannie and gave her a slight nod. Beside her was the table with the candle still burning next to the picture of Amy's grandfather. But the floor was covered with boxes and books and piles of clothes.

"Amy, are you moving again?" Jeannie asked in surprise. Then she clapped her hands happily. "Oh, are you coming back to Hollywood? Miss Morgan must have found you after all!"

Amy and her mother exchanged glances. "I guess you haven't heard yet," Amy said.

"Heard what?" Jeannie asked, frowning.

Amy sighed. "President Roosevelt has ordered all Japanese and Japanese-Americans to leave the West Coast until the war is over. People say it's for our own safety," she added in a low voice, "but they're really afraid we're all enemy spies."

"Amy, don't talk like that," Mrs. Mochida said sharply. "It is our duty to follow the president's order. That is how we can prove our loyalty to this country."

Amy bent down and picked up a record from the floor. Then she let it drop again, and the record shattered.

"Amy!" Her mother sounded shocked. "That is quite enough!" She gave Amy a warning look and began to sort through a stack of kitchen utensils.

"Who cares if everything gets smashed now?" Amy said, giving one of the record pieces a kick. "We're going to have to throw away most of our stuff anyway. Or give it to all those horrible people who keep coming by to see if they can have our things." She nodded toward a pile of boxes, and her eyes filled with angry tears. "We can't take very much with us," she told Jeannie. "Only what we can manage to carry ourselves. And we have to take towels and pots and blankets."

"That's terrible!" Jeannie cried. "Can't you just give things to someone to keep for you?"

Amy sighed. "There's hardly anyone left in Little Tokyo anymore. And we have to report to the train station early tomorrow morning. Tad and his grandfather are going with us."

"But where are you going?" Jeannie asked, beginning to panic. How could this be happening?

"We don't really know," Amy said. "People are saying that we're being sent to special camps in the middle of nowhere. It sounds like we're going to be prisoners of war."

Jeannie sank down on the floor. "It's like some awful nightmare," she said.

"I guess my mother is right. It's the only way we can prove our loyalty to other Americans," Amy said. "Maybe it won't be so bad."

Jeannie didn't think her friend sounded very hopeful. She reached into her schoolbag. "I have something for you," she said, slowly taking out the picture of Clark Gable. "But I guess it doesn't seem so important anymore."

Amy smiled sadly and took the photograph. "It is important," she said. "I'm going to take it with me, so I can remember all the good times we had together. Where did you get it?"

"From Miss Morgan," Jeannie said. "She didn't know how to find you. And you know what? She wanted you and your mother to come back."

Amy's tears were spilling over now. "I wish we could go back to Hollywood," she said. "But it's too late now."

Jeannie nodded glumly. Then she said, "Well, there's one bit of good news, anyway. Miss Morgan threw that awful Mr. Whick out of the house."

"Good," Amy said, sniffing. "It serves him right."

"Amy, it's getting late," Mrs. Mochida called from across the room. She was packing Oba San's brightly colored kimonos into a black trunk. "We still have a lot to do."

"I'd better get home anyway," Jeannie said

reluctantly. "It'll be dark soon."

"Wait a minute," Amy said. She ran into the other room and came back with a small, flat box tied with a pink ribbon. She handed the box to Jeannie.

"What is it?" Jeannie asked.

"My movie-star album," Amy said. "I was going to send it to you. I want you to have it."

"Thanks, Amy," Jeannie said. It was hard to get the words out because there was a huge lump forming in her throat. "I'll keep it for you until you come back."

Once again, Jeannie had to say good-bye to the Mochidas. And this time, it was even harder. This time, she wasn't sure she would ever see Amy again.

Maybe the war would be over soon, and Amy and her mother would move back to Hollywood. Maybe she and Amy could be best friends again. Maybe they could laugh and go to the movies together, just like before.

"We're Going to Be Prisoners of War"

But as Jeannie stepped out into the deserted, darkening streets of Little Tokyo, she knew one thing for sure. No matter what happened, things would never be quite the same.

Amy, Jeannie, and the other characters in this story are fictional, but the historical events in *American Dreams* really took place.

Two months after the Japanese attack on Pearl Harbor on December 7, 1941, the President of the United States, Franklin D. Roosevelt, signed Executive Order 9066. This order forced 112,000 people of Japanese descent, including American citizens, to leave their homes on the West Coast for special relocation camps located farther inland. Many people, including some important government leaders, believed that Japanese-Americans might be spying for the Japanese, and that they therefore posed a threat to U.S. security. An agency called the War Relocation Authority, or

Historical Postscript

Having gathered their belongings for a hasty journey from their homes, Japanese-American families often found themselves subjected to random searches.

WRA, was formed to direct the removal of Japanese-American men, women, and children.

First, the Japanese-Americans were assigned numbers and sent to fifteen "assembly centers" set up along the coast. These centers were usually racetracks or fairgrounds that had been hastily made into barracks. The living conditions in these assembly centers were terrible. The camps were heavily guarded and surrounded by barbed wire, and the people inside were not allowed to leave. Food was in short supply, and the conditions were often unsanitary. People had to line up to use the toilets and laundry tubs, and there were no doors in the lavatories. Some internees slept in converted stables, and the barracks were extremely crowded. There was no privacy for anyone, and the FBI made regular searches of the barracks, looking for illegal items such as radios, cameras, and

Courtesy of the Library of Congress

Like the parcels they're sitting on, two young Japanese-American boys are tagged for identification during the relocation process.

weapons. The entire experience was frightening and humiliating for the Japanese-American prisoners. But many of them felt that they were proving their loyalty to their

Courtesy of the Library of Congress

Temporary detention centers, quickly constructed, offered little privacy, protection, or space.

country by living quietly in the camps.

A few months later, as the Japanese-Americans were trying to adjust to their new quarters, they had to move again. This time, they were sent to "relocation camps" in faraway states. These new camps were located in remote areas, such as deserts, where the authorities thought that the prisoners could not cause trouble. The conditions in some of these camps were even worse than those in the assembly centers.

Some people claimed that the Japanese-Americans were better off in these camps—safe from other Americans who might want to retaliate for the attack on Pearl Harbor. There were rumors, many of them printed in the newspapers, that Japanese-Americans had been operating secret radio stations and signaling Japanese submarines off the coast at night with flashlights. One newspaper even reported that the caps on the tomatoes in a Japanese farmer's field pointed toward an American air base.

Some people defended the Japanese-Americans. They said that holding these people prisoner was unfair and a violation of the Constitution. After all, many of the prisoners were American citizens, and none of them had been accused of any crimes. In fact, no Japanese- American was ever found guilty of any crimes against the United States during this period. But because it

Courtesy of the Library of Congress

It was difficult to hang onto clothing, family photos, and personal mementos when trunks and bags were heaped together at the internment camps.

was wartime, and because so many other Americans were frightened and angry, the constitutional rights of the Japanese-Americans were suspended.

Most Japanese-Americans remained in the desolate internment camps until the end of the war. Every day, they raised the flag, said the Pledge of Allegiance, and stood at attention while the drum-and-bugle corps played "The Star Spangled Banner." Eventually, some of the prisoners, particularly college students, were allowed to leave, if the authorities decided that they did not pose a threat to the country. One way young Japanese-American men could get out of the camps was to join the United States Army. To become soldiers, they had to take special loyalty oaths. And they had to join Japanese-only regiments. Some young men were resentful that they were being asked to serve a country that didn't treat them as citizens. But others felt that by joining the army they could prove their loyalty to the United States. Most Japanese-American soldiers belonged to the 100/442nd Regimental Combat Team. That unit won more medals for bravery than any other American outfit in World War II.

In 1976, more than thirty years after the Japanese-Americans were sent to the internment camps, the United States government finally admitted that it had violated the rights and liberties of Japanese-Americans. President Gerald Ford said that "Japanese-Americans were and are loyal Americans." And six years later, after a long study, a group commissioned by President Carter decided that the Japanese-Americans imprisoned in camps during World War II had been treated unfairly. It blamed the whole fiasco on prejudice against the Japanese, war hysteria, and government leaders of the time.

In 1988, a Redress Bill was passed by Congress. Its purpose was to give money to the Japanese-Americans who had suffered in the camps. Many of them had lost their homes and all of their savings. But this bill came too late for many of the Japanese-American prisoners, who had already died.

The United States Constitution guarantees the same rights and freedoms to every citizen. But back in the 1940s, the civil rights movement had not yet taken place. Few people seemed to care that the civil rights of the Japanese-Americans were being ignored. Now, we probably find it hard to imagine that so many people could be treated so unfairly, but, as Jeannie learned in the story, fairness and equality are things we have to pay attention to all the time.

To Learn More about Japanese-Americans, Check Out...

Japanese American Journey: The Story of a People. [San Mateo: Japanese-American Curriculum Project, Inc., 1985.]

Kitano, Harry. *The Japanese Americans*. [New York: Chelsea House Publishers, 1987.]

Leathers, Noel L. *The Japanese in America*. [Lerner Publications Co., 1991.]

Stein, R. Conrad. *World at War: The Home Front*. [Chicago: Children's Press, 1986.]

Stein, R. Conrad. *World at War: Nisei Regiment*. [Chicago: Children's Press, 1985.]

Uchida, Yoshiko. *The Invisible Thread*. [Englewood Cliffs, NJ: Julian Messner, 1991.]

Other Books in the **STORIES OF THE STATES** series

*Drums at Saratoga**
by Lisa Banim

*East Side Story**
*Golden Quest**
by Bonnie Bader

Fire in the Valley
*Mr. Peale's Bones**
*Voyage of the Half Moon**
by Tracey West

Forbidden Friendship
by Judy Eichler Weber

Children of Flight Pedro Pan
by Maria Armengol Acierno

A Message for General Washington
by Vivian Schurfranz

*Available in paperback

If you are interested in ordering other **STORIES OF THE STATES** books, please call Silver Moon Press at our **toll free** number (800) 874-3320 for ordering information.